TAKE THE COURT

Check out these other L'il D books!

#1 It's All in the Name

Coming soon:

#3 Stuck in the Middle

Hey L'il D!
TAKE THE COURT

By Bob Lanier
and Heather Goodyear

Illustrated by
Desire Grover

A
LITTLE APPLE
PAPERBACK

SCHOLASTIC INC.
New York   Toronto   London   Auckland   Sydney
Mexico City   New Delhi   Hong Kong   Buenos Aires

I'd like to dedicate this book to my lovely wife, Rosegina, and thank her for her special gifts of love and patience during this process. And a special thanks to my daughter Kahori and son Kamal for sharing some of their pearls of wisdom about school experiences with me. With all my love, always.
— B. L.

For my mom and dad — you love and guide me.
— H. G.

ISBN 0-439-40900-4
Text copyright © 2003 by Bob Lanier
Illustrations copyright © 2003 by Scholastic Inc.
All rights reserved. Published by Scholastic Inc.
SCHOLASTIC, LITTLE APPLE, and
associated logos are trademarks and/or registered
trademarks of Scholastic Inc.

12 11 10 9 8 7 6 5 4 3   4 5 6 7 8/0

Printed in the U.S.A.
First printing, April 2003

Dear Reader,

Thank you for picking up this book. It's all about when I was a kid — back when people called me L'il Dobber, instead of Big Bob. Back before I played in the NBA.

I grew up in Buffalo, New York. I loved basketball and played every chance I got. Luckily, I had great friends to hang out with both on and off the court. We had a lot of fun adventures — and they're all included in these books.

Soon you'll meet me as a kid (remember, they call me L'il Dobber!). You'll also meet my friends, Joe, Sam, and Gan. We are always up to something! We may not do the right thing all the time, but whatever we do, we learn from it. And we have a lot of fun.

And that's something I hope you do with this HEY L'IL D! book — have fun. Because believe me, reading is one of the most fun, most important things that you can do.

I hope you like my story.

Bob Lanier

Contents

Chapter 1
Their Court

L'il Dobber bounced the basketball to Sam. She dribbled around her twin brother, Joe, and shot a basket from a few feet back.

"Good shot," L'il Dobber yelled to Sam over the recess noise. Kids shouted on the playground and traffic buzzed outside the school fence.

L'il Dobber and his friends, Joe, Gan, and Sam, were playing a game of two-on-two at the only hoop and painted key in the cement school yard. This small court was the site of the daily lunchtime games they enjoyed so much.

L'il Dobber was stepping up to guard Gan when he saw Brooks and his three side-kicks walk up to the side of the court.

What's he going to bug me about now? wondered L'il Dobber.

"Hey, Feet," Brooks said to L'il Dobber. "We've decided we might try playing here at recess."

The two-on-two game stopped.

"You can't decide that. The court is ours at recess," L'il Dobber said to Brooks.

"Says who?"

"Yeah, says who?" asked his sidekicks.

"We've had it every day this year," L'il Dobber exclaimed.

"It's almost a lunch recess rule," Sam said, walking up to stand next to L'il Dobber.

"Rules can change," Brooks said.

He glanced at his buddies, and they all walked away to the other side of the school yard.

"What did he mean?" asked Joe after they'd gone.

"I don't know," Gan said.

L'il Dobber shook his head. "And I don't want to find out."

L'il Dobber walked out the metal door to lunch recess two days later and stopped so quickly that Joe and Gan ran right into his back.

"What's going on?" L'il Dobber yelled in shock.

Brooks and his sidekicks were grouped under the basket, shooting hoops.

L'il Dobber, Joe, and Gan ran over to the small court.

"What are you guys doing?" demanded L'il Dobber.

"Playing a little hoops, Feet," Brooks said, as if they did it every day.

"Obviously," said Brooks's pals together.

"*We* play here at recess," L'il Dobber told them.

"Not today," said Brooks. He caught the next pass and held the ball at his side.

"Yeah," the sidekicks agreed.

"And not until we want to give up the court," said Brooks.

"Yeah," the pals said again.

"I hear hopscotch is open," Brooks said to L'il Dobber. "You could draw the squares bigger so your feet will fit inside."

Sam ran up just as Brooks and his buddies started tossing the basketball again.

"What's going on here?" Sam demanded.

Brooks dribbled the ball in place and stared at Sam.

"Feet can clue you in," he said to her.

"Don't call L'il Dobber, 'Feet,' " Sam said angrily. Then she turned to her friends. "What's going on?"

"Brooks and his pals think they're going to take over the court at recess," said L'il Dobber.

"Why?" Sam asked Brooks. "You don't like basketball as much as we do."

"No, but I like taking the court away from you guys," said Brooks.

Ms. Grant, the recess attendant, came

over to the two groups glaring at each other on the court.

"Do I need to settle something between you guys today?" she asked.

Brooks looked at L'il Dobber, challenging him to get Ms. Grant to help them.

"No, we're all set," L'il Dobber said. It was like a playground code — they would try to fix the problem by themselves before getting a teacher involved.

"Let's go, guys," L'il Dobber said miserably.

He turned and dribbled his basketball over to the fence. Joe, Sam, and Gan followed. They all sat down and leaned their backs against the jangling metal. Waiting out the rest of lunch recess, they stared at what they had always believed was *their* court.

Chapter 2
L'il D's Lowdown

After school, L'il Dobber dribbled his basketball on the sidewalk along the busy main drag of Northland Avenue. He and Gan were walking together.

"Science was cool today," said Gan looking up at the sky. Their class had just started a unit on weather. "Are those clouds cirrus or cumulus?"

"L'il Dobber!"

Before he could answer Gan, L'il Dobber turned to see Joe and Sam running up behind them.

"Hey, guys," Joe and Sam greeted them when they caught up.

"Hey," they answered, and they all fell into step together.

"We were talking about science," said L'il Dobber. "What kind of clouds are those, Joe?"

Joe looked up at the sky. "Cumulus," he said.

"Those are the ones that rain," said Gan.

"I hope they don't rain out the park on Saturday," L'il Dobber said.

"Why?" asked Gan.

"Because park season started last week," L'il Dobber answered.

"Oh, that's right!" Sam said excitedly. "Tell us about it."

"Saturday was a big opening day," L'il Dobber said.

"What's park season?" Gan asked.

"See, you don't know since you just moved here," L'il Dobber explained. "But park season is big in the neighborhood."

"Yeah, every Saturday morning in the fall, the basketball court at Como Park is filled with guys waiting to play," Joe explained.

"Guys like us?" asked Gan.

"No way," said L'il Dobber. "Players who are famous around here. Like old high school players and guys who are on the high school and college teams now."

"L'il Dobber's dad always plays and so he gets to go and watch," Sam said.

"Why would you want to watch them play?" asked Gan.

"Because they're the best players in the city," said L'il Dobber. "I can't wait to play in the games when I'm older."

"Me, either," said Joe.

"I wish we could go sometime," Sam said, "but Mom always likes to spend Saturdays with Joe and me."

The group walked on quietly for a few minutes until L'il Dobber had an idea. "Hey! I could keep you guys posted on the games. Like a sports recap on Mondays," he said.

"You could call your report to us 'L'il D's Lowdown,'" Sam said enthusiastically.

"You could watch for something different each week and tell us the stats," Joe said, joining in the excitement.

L'il Dobber was pleased with his plan. "What should I look for first?" he asked.

"How about longest run?" suggested Joe.

"Run?" Gan asked. "Don't they just run up and down the court? That's not very far."

L'il Dobber, Joe, and Sam laughed good-naturedly at Gan's question.

Then Joe quickly cleared up the confusion. "Not a run like distance. A *run* is who gets to play the most games in a row."

"Oh," said Gan.

"See, your team has to win to stay on the court and play the next game," L'il Dobber explained, "so if you have a long run, you get to play a lot."

"And it means your team keeps winning," Joe said.

"It also means you're a good player," said L'il Dobber. "And a player who can win games at the park can win games anywhere."

Chapter 3
Playing Like Dit

On Saturday, L'il Dobber dribbled his basketball along the sidelines of the court at Como Park. The bottom rows of the bleachers were filled with guys waiting to play. Above them sat a large crowd of neighborhood people talking and watching the game.

The games were always really exciting to L'il Dobber, but especially when his dad was playing. Dit had been a basketball star at Bennett High School, and L'il Dobber wanted to be just like him.

Dit was the reason for his nickname — L'il Dobber. Adults all called Dit "Big Dobber." Hardly anyone ever called L'il Dobber by his real name, Bob Lanier, anymore. He was L'il Dobber, and he was aiming to be just like Big Dobber.

"Nice defense, Dit!" L'il Dobber called out as his dad stole the ball from the other team and sprinted down for an easy bucket.

As the other team was bringing the ball back up the court, L'il Dobber heard someone shout, "Zelly Dow is in the house!"

He turned from the game for a minute to watch Zelly Dow approach. Zelly was a former high school star, like Dit. He was a great player, but he bragged way too much. The games always heated up when Zelly was on the court.

Zelly walked to the side of the bleachers. "Who's captain of the next team?" he asked the group of guys sitting there in gym shorts and sneakers.

One of the high school players nervously said, "I — I — I am, Mr. Dow. Would you like to play?"

"Cool," answered Zelly as he unzipped his duffel bag and pulled out a pair of sneakers.

L'il Dobber turned his attention back to the game as Zelly began to stretch.

Dit was dribbling down the court. An opponent stepped in, stole the ball, and headed to the other end for a layup.

Dit's not going to be happy about that play, thought L'il Dobber.

Immediately, Dit's friend and teammate Clyde Alexander, got the rebound, dribbled down the court, and scored.

The game was tied at fourteen to fourteen. One more point for either team and the game was over.

Dit caught the ball. Clyde Alexander ran under the basket and Dit hit him with a bounce pass. Clyde slammed the ball through the hoop and yelled, "Game time!" They'd won!

"Who's got *next*?" Dit called toward the bleachers.

The team that had been playing Dit's left the court. As Zelly Dow's team came out to play, the crowd cheered him on.

Zelly Dow had been playing against Dit and Clyde Alexander since high school, when

he was on another school's team. Zelly and Clyde always played extra hard trying to beat each other, so the crowd was expecting a great game.

L'il Dobber dribbled along the sideline to be as close as possible to the action.

Dit's team played hard but couldn't recover after falling four points behind at the very beginning. In fact, the game never got very exciting after all, since Dit's team got creamed.

"Fifteen!" yelled Zelly's team as they sank the last basket. Dit was done for the day.

"That was a good run today, Dit," L'il Dobber told his dad as they walked away from the bleachers.

"Thanks," said Dit. "I had strong players on my team."

"Too bad you lost to Zelly Dow though," said L'il Dobber.

"I guess it was his week to win," said Dit. "Maybe next week it will be mine."

L'il Dobber was always disappointed when Dit's team lost. But as they left the park gate, he was excited thinking about the drive home. Next to watching the games, the best part of Saturdays for L'il Dobber was talking with Dit about every game detail the whole way home.

Chapter 4
A Real Jersey

The sidewalk grew more crowded as L'il Dobber, Joe, and Gan got closer to school on Monday morning. Being a half-foot taller than any other kid, L'il Dobber looked over a bunch of them and saw Brooks coming across the street. His three sidekicks were right beside him.

Brooks was wearing an authentic NBA New York Knicks jersey.

The fall morning was cold enough that all the kids had on jackets — except for Brooks.

Probably because it would cover up his jersey, L'il Dobber thought.

"What are you staring at, Feet?" Brooks asked L'il Dobber rudely as he came up next to him on the sidewalk.

"Just your jersey," L'il Dobber had to admit, trying to keep the envy out of his voice.

"I know. It's sweet," said Brooks.

He held his arms out at his sides to model his new shirt.

"Very sweet," agreed Brooks's buddies.

"You think you're so great at basketball, Feet. Too bad you don't have one," Brooks said.

"I will when I play in the NBA," L'il Dobber said confidently. "With my own name and number on the back."

"Maybe I'll have my name on a jersey someday, too," Joe said to stick up for L'il Dobber.

"Me, too," agreed Gan.

"We'll all be famous players and then you can buy *our* jerseys to wear," Joe told Brooks.

L'il Dobber and Gan nodded and smiled at Joe, but Brooks laughed loudly. Then his buddies joined in.

"Sure," Brooks said. "Gan Xu, short guy with thick glasses; Bob Lanier, with the big feet; and Joe Crantz, slow as a turtle. There's a triple threat for any basketball team!"

Brooks and his buddies were still laughing as they came to the last corner on the way to school where L'il Dobber's mom worked as the crossing guard.

Brooks usually stopped his teasing before they got to Mrs. Lanier. But today he was having such a good laugh he forgot where he was on the street.

"Hi, Mom," L'il Dobber said quietly.

"Good morning, everyone," Mrs. Lanier

said. She turned to the group as they waited for a break in the busy traffic.

Mrs. Lanier looked at the scowl on L'il Dobber's face. He often confided to his mom

about Brooks's teasing, and she guessed that Brooks's laughter was aimed at L'il Dobber.

"How nice to see all of you walking together today," Mrs. Lanier said. "Brooks, the way you're laughing, you must have had a *fun* weekend."

"Not really," Brooks said. He stopped laughing and elbowed his buddies to get them to stop, too. "I was just laughing."

"I see," said Mrs. Lanier. She eyed Brooks for another second. Then the traffic paused, and she held up her small stop sign and stepped into the street.

"You all have a good day, now," she told the group as they moved past her.

She smiled and gave L'il Dobber's shoulder a quick squeeze on his way past.

"I'll see you at home, Bobby," she said.

Brooks walked faster to get ahead of L'il Dobber as they crossed the street and walked into school. L'il Dobber could still see the back of Brooks's jersey and the big number twenty. He'd remember to never pick that number for himself when he played in the NBA.

*   *   *

L'il Dobber stood outside with Joe at lunch recess. They took turns practicing spinning the basketball on their fingertips. They had looked around for something else to do, but nothing seemed fun when Brooks was playing ball on the court.

"Let's meet at Delaware Park after school so *we* get a chance to shoot some hoops," Joe suggested as he tossed the ball to L'il Dobber. They liked to play ball at a local park after school whenever they were allowed. Today was the perfect day, too, since they couldn't play at recess.

"I bet I can go," replied L'il Dobber as he caught the ball tumbling off his fingers. The idea made L'il Dobber feel a little bit better.

"I'll be there after I call and check in with my mom at work," said Joe.

"We'll ask Gan, too, if he comes back to school today," said L'il Dobber.

"I wonder where he went," said Joe.

"I don't know," said L'il Dobber. "What about Sam? Will she play?"

"Of course she'll play."

Sam was across the school yard jumping rope double-dutch with some other fourth grade girls.

"She doesn't seem to be missing basketball as much as us," L'il Dobber commented.

"She is," Joe said. "She's lucky, though,

because she has stuff she can do with girls when she's not playing ball with us. Last night at home she told me she wished Brooks would get off the court so we could play again."

"Hey, guys," yelled Gan as he came running across the school yard.

"Where have you been?" asked L'il Dobber, dribbling the ball with his left hand.

"I had a fun rest of the morning. My mom dropped off my two brothers at the dentist while she took my sisters and me to the eye doctor. And I got to go out to lunch."

"The eye doctor doesn't sound like fun. Out to lunch sounds pretty good, though," said L'il Dobber.

"Even the eye doctor would have been better than standing here and watching Brooks and his buddies," said Joe.

Gan smiled. "You didn't tell us about Como Park this morning," he said. "Give us 'L'il D's Lowdown.'"

L'il Dobber held onto his basketball. "The longest run was seven games," he said.

"Dit's team had a run of five games. Then he got beat by a team Zelly Dow was on."

"Who's Zelly Dow?" asked Gan.

"Dit and his friend Clyde Alexander played against Zelly Dow in high school," L'il Dobber said.

"I remember you said last year that Clyde Alexander and Zelly Dow don't like to lose to each other," said Joe.

L'il Dobber nodded and tossed the ball to Gan. "Right," he said. "Dit told me they've never gotten along."

"Sounds a lot like you and Brooks," said Gan, flipping the ball up onto his finger.

"Exactly," said L'il Dobber. "If Brooks and I played in the park games, I know we wouldn't want to lose to each other, either."

Chapter 5
Clyde and Zelly

"Bobby, if you put any bigger spoonfuls in your mouth, you'll choke," Mrs. Lanier said to L'il Dobber.

L'il Dobber knew he would get in trouble for sassing his mom if he tried to say he was eating fast because the food was so good. The truth was, even though she made terrific grits and eggs, he was really eating fast so he could get to Como Park.

"You could just lick it off your plate and not waste time with a spoon," his older sister, Geraldine, said.

L'il Dobber ignored Geraldine's comment and tried to take a smaller bite of eggs.

"I need to . . ." he began saying.

"Please chew your food and then speak," his mother told him.

L'il Dobber swallowed and then said, "I need to be ready when Dit gets back from the car wash. We left late last week and it took forever for him to get on the court."

"Your dad won't be home for another twenty minutes. You have time to eat with good manners."

"The way these games are so important to these men," Mrs. Lanier continued, "you'd think they were the NBA finals."

"It's really the one thing that won't be so great about playing in the NBA," L'il Dobber said thoughtfully.

"What's that?" asked his mother.

"I'll have to stop playing at Como Park. I'll already be in preseason with my team at this time of the year."

"I don't think you need to get disappointed yet," Geraldine said and looked at L'il Dobber across the kitchen table. "I haven't noticed any professional teams calling you about playing for them."

"Of course not," L'il Dobber shot back. "I can't get drafted out of the fourth grade, Jerdine."

"Let's just wait until your senior year of college before hearing about your draft potential," said Mrs. Lanier, putting an end to the conversation before it turned into an argument.

Mrs. Lanier eyed the large bite L'il Dobber was about to spoon into his mouth. "And if you choke on your food before then, you'll have bigger worries than your draft number."

*   *   *

An hour later, L'il Dobber and Dit ar-
rived at Como Park.

"Clyde, how you doing today, man?" Dit
said as they reached the bleachers

"Decent, Big Dobber," Clyde Alexander

replied. "How about you?" The two friends reached out and punched fists in greeting. "And how you doing, L'il Dobber? Gonna hang out on our sidelines again today?"

L'il Dobber tilted his head back to look up at Clyde Alexander.

"You bet," said L'il Dobber.

"Maybe we can get a run together today, Clyde," Dit said.

"Absolutely. You'll be the fifth on my team and we've got next."

L'il Dobber was excited that Dit would be on the court for the next game.

"I hope Zelly's team gets knocked off the court this time," Clyde said. "I have a hard time holding my temper with him."

"Next!" came the call from the court. Zelly Dow's team had won.

L'il Dobber dribbled over to the side of the court. The game was very fast paced.

Clyde scored most of the points for Dit's team. Zelly Dow was guarding Clyde, and L'il Dobber watched him get angrier each time

Clyde scored. When Zelly's team finally lost, Zelly walked off the court glaring at Clyde.

L'il Dobber stopped cheering for Dit's team as Zelly brushed by to collect his things. Then he watched as Zelly left the park, slamming the gate shut behind him.

Chapter 6
A Plan

"I was watching for ball-handling skills this week," L'il Dobber reported to Joe and Gan as they sat by the fence at recess on Monday. "There were some good moves. I'll show you one Clyde Alexander used."

L'il Dobber stood up and had Joe and Gan stand in front of him so the three of them made a triangle.

"Pretend I'm dribbling toward the basket and you two are on my team," he said.

L'il Dobber dribbled close to Gan and away from Joe.

"See, this is how Clyde made the other team come over to guard him."

Then L'il Dobber spun around Gan. As he came around in the spin, he passed the ball across to Joe.

"The other team is looking at me and so, when I spin behind Gan, Joe is open," said L'il Dobber.

"That's a good move," agreed Gan. "Let me try."

L'il Dobber, Gan, and Joe took turns practicing. Timing the pass just right was the hard part. Quite a few throws went wild when the boys spun too fast.

The whistle blew to end recess. L'il Dobber kept the ball and dribbled across the playground on their way back into school.

"I'll tell ya'," he said to Joe and Gan as they walked down the hall to their classroom, "Zelly Dow and Clyde Alexander are getting madder and madder at each other on the court. By the end of the game on Saturday, they were almost wrestling under the baskets."

"Maybe you should watch for fouls this week," said Joe.

"I could give you a whole 'Lowdown' on just the ones between Zelly Dow and Clyde Alexander."

That evening, the Laniers were eating dinner at their kitchen table and talking about the day. Geraldine had done well on a sixth grade science quiz about plants, so she was teaching them about each vegetable in

Mrs. Lanier's homemade soup. She told them they were eating a lot of roots and tubers.

I call them turnips and potatoes, thought L'il Dobber.

Near the end of the meal, L'il Dobber's dad asked him about basketball at school.

"You haven't said much about lunchtime basketball lately."

"We haven't been playing since Brooks and his three buddies took over the court and won't give it back."

"When did this happen?"

"A couple weeks ago."

"Couldn't you all try to play together?" asked Mrs. Lanier.

"I don't think so," said L'il Dobber.

"Why not? It would be nice if you could all try to work it out," said his mom.

"You know Brooks," said L'il Dobber. "He won't share. Maybe other kids, but not Brooks."

"Well, that is too bad. I know how much you like to play ball each day," Mrs. Lanier said.

"Joe says we should just walk up and push them off the court," said L'il Dobber.

Dit put his fork down and stared straight at L'il Dobber. "You know your mother and I don't approve of you fighting. You stand your ground, but you don't start fights," he said.

"None of us can think of anything else, though," said L'il Dobber. He was hoping maybe his parents would have some ideas.

"Try to wait it out," said Mrs. Lanier.

"We've been waiting for a long time," complained L'il Dobber.

"I bet they want to bother you more than they want to play basketball." Dit said. "Try to be cool and make them think you don't care."

"OK," agreed L'il Dobber. "We'll try that tomorrow."

On their way out to the school yard the next day at lunch, L'il Dobber told Joe and Gan, "Remember to be cool and ignore them if they get the court today."

They walked out the lunchroom door and saw Brooks and his buddies bouncing a ball on the court and watching for them.

Instead of walking over to the fence to sit, L'il Dobber stopped right by the court.

"Hey, Feet," said Brooks.

L'il Dobber ignored him and said to Joe and Gan, "Let's dribble the ball around right here."

He tossed the ball to Joe.

"Hey, Feet," Brooks said louder.

L'il Dobber didn't look at him.

"Hey, Feet!" called Brooks's sidekicks even louder.

L'il Dobber caught a pass back from Joe, dribbled a few feet along the side of the court, and passed the ball to Gan.

"It's hard to play without a basket," Brooks said. "Too bad we've got the only one."

Ignore him, L'il Dobber kept repeating to himself. He jogged around to the other side of the court and Gan threw him the ball.

"Don't get dizzy running around the court in your little circle," Brooks said. "Since you won't be doing any running *on* the court," he added and laughed.

I've had enough, thought L'il Dobber. He picked up his dribble, stuck the ball under his arm, and went to spend recess by the fence again.

After school, L'il Dobber walked in the back door and found his mom and Geraldine having a snack in the kitchen.

"I tried ignoring Brooks and his buddies today, but it didn't work," he said and flopped down into one of the chairs at the table.

"Joe and Gan and I even dribbled around right next to the court and pretended Brooks wasn't there."

"And what did they do then?" Geraldine asked.

"Brooks just kept saying stuff to me until I didn't want to take it anymore and we went and sat by the fence again."

"I'm sorry, Bobby," said his mom. "You might just have to wait until Brooks is tired of playing basketball every day."

"How did they get the court from you, anyway?" Geraldine asked.

"We came out from lunch one day and they were already there."

"So beat them out to the court after lunch," said Geraldine, as if L'il Dobber had missed the obvious answer to his problem.

L'il Dobber smiled. "That sounds easy," he said.

Chapter 7
Closer to the Court

"Eat your lunches fast!" L'il Dobber said to Joe and Gan at the lunch table. "We're going to beat Brooks to the court today."

"We've tried for three days," Gan said, chewing a mouthful of carrots. "If we have to keep doing this every day I'm going to tell my mom to pack soup and pudding."

"Yeah. Nothing you have to chew for a long time," said Joe.

L'il Dobber, Joe, and Gan finished their lunches and still had four minutes to sit at the table and watch the clock.

At 11:35 sharp, they jumped up and sprinted toward the playground door. They

pushed through the other kids trying to get outside.

"Slow down!" yelled the lunchroom attendant.

L'il Dobber slowed to a fast walk for his last three strides to the door. He stopped when he stepped outside and looked at the court.

"It didn't work," L'il Dobber said sadly.

"Brooks is already there again," Gan said.

"Oh, well," said Joe as they walked across the school yard. "I want to sit down, anyway. My stomach hurts from eating so fast."

L'il Dobber went straight home after school to find his mom and Geraldine.

"We tried," L'il Dobber said as he grabbed an apple off the table for a snack. "But Brooks is already outside when we get out the door."

"There's your real problem then," said Geraldine.

"What?" asked L'il Dobber.

"Figure out how Brooks is getting to the court so fast and you'll be playing basketball again in no time," stated Geraldine matter-of-factly.

Later that night, L'il Dobber thought about what Geraldine had said and realized it might be her best idea yet.

L'il Dobber, Joe, and Gan kept an eye on Brooks the next day while they ate their lunches. One minute before it was time to go outside, Brooks walked up to one of the lunchroom attendants, said something, and hurried out the door to the school yard.

The three friends got up one minute later, rushed outside, and, sure enough, Brooks was on the court.

"He's got some trick he's doing," said Joe as they walked past the court without looking at Brooks.

"How are we going to figure out what that trick is?" Gan asked.

L'il Dobber sat down on his basketball

by the fence while Brooks's sidekicks walked onto the court to play.

"I guess we've got another whole recess to think about it," he said as he watched Brooks throw a shot toward the basket.

Swish! The ball fell through the hoop as L'il Dobber's shoulders slumped down in defeat.

At lunch the next day, L'il Dobber heard "Bob Lanier!" yelled over the lunchroom noise. He walked up to the lunchroom attendant who had called him, and she handed him some forms about the new crossing duty times to take home to his mom. As he turned to go sit down again, Brooks walked up to the attendant.

"You may go out to help Ms. Grant ready the playground, Brooks," the attendant said.

"Do what?" L'il Dobber asked Brooks.

"I've got to go, man — Ms. Grant's waiting for me," Brooks said hurriedly and ran out the door to the school yard.

Wow, he's slick, thought L'il Dobber as

he went back to the lunch table to tell Joe and Gan what he had heard.

L'il Dobber, Sam, Gan, and Joe were sitting in a circle by the school yard fence as far away as possible from the basketball court. They tried to talk quietly while they planned what they would do about their discovery.

"Brooks is a liar," L'il Dobber concluded after telling Sam what had happened earlier in the lunchroom. "I don't think he's out here helping Ms. Grant at all."

"How can we find out for sure?" asked Sam.

"And what do we do about it?" chimed in Gan.

"I still say we just go fight them for the court," said Joe.

"No. I would be in big trouble at home if I got in a fight," said Gan.

"Me, too," agreed L'il Dobber.

"We could ask Ms. Grant about it," Sam suggested.

"Who should ask her?" Joe wondered.

"Gan should," said L'il Dobber right away.

"I should?" asked Gan. "Why?"

"She trusts you, since you told the truth about that car accident a few weeks ago," L'il

Dobber answered, and nodded toward the stoplight at the corner. "Ms. Grant wouldn't think you were making up a story."

"Okay, I guess," said Gan. "When should I ask her?"

"Now might be good," answered L'il Dobber. He pointed toward the monkey bars, where Ms. Grant was standing by herself.

"The sooner you do, the sooner we won't have to sit here at recess anymore," said Joe.

Gan stood up from their circle and walked over to Ms. Grant. She listened and smiled at him. L'il Dobber hoped this meant she was believing him. Gan turned and ran back to them.

"What'd she say?" L'il Dobber asked anxiously.

"She said she'll talk to Brooks tomorrow since recess is almost over."

"Did she believe you?" asked Sam.

"I think so."

"Woo-hoo! We'll be playing basketball again tomorrow!" Joe yelled.

"Shh!" Gan whispered loudly and looked over at the court.

"I hope we will be," said L'il Dobber. "Thanks for talking to Ms. Grant, Gan."

The whistle blew for the end of lunch recess and L'il Dobber grabbed his basketball. For the first time since Brooks and his buddies had taken over the court, he felt excited thinking about the next day's recess.

Chapter 8
Brooks Gets Busted

L'il Dobber, Joe, Gan, and Sam watched Brooks leave through the school yard door one minute early at lunch the next day.

Ms. Grant was speaking to Brooks by the basketball court when they got out. She waved for them to come over.

"I was just asking Brooks why he and his friends have started playing basketball every day," Ms. Grant told them.

"We like it," said Brooks.

"I see. L'il Dobber, Joe, Gan, and Sam really like it, too, don't you think?" asked Ms. Grant.

Brooks shrugged. "I guess."

"I've noticed you seem to be just a few steps ahead of them coming out to the court at recess. How does that happen?"

"I don't know," Brooks answered, while his eyes focused on his buddies approaching the court. He wouldn't look directly at Ms. Grant.

"I must eat lunch faster, maybe."

"Let me ask you again, Brooks," Ms. Grant said. She waited until Brooks was looking at her and then continued, "Before you answer this time, I'll tell you I talked to the lunchroom attendants after recess yesterday."

"Well . . ." Brooks said.

"You lied, didn't you, Brooks?"

"Yes," he admitted hesitantly, knowing he was caught.

"Do you really think it's OK to lie at school, or anywhere for that matter?" questioned Ms. Grant with a very stern voice.

"No, ma'am," responded Brooks.

"I truly hope not," Ms. Grant replied. "I also hope you will never try to lie again to the adults who are here at school to take care of you."

"Yes, ma'am," repeated Brooks quietly, and he began to fidget with the basketball in his hands.

L'il Dobber was a little uncomfortable being this close to another kid who was getting in trouble. But since it was Brooks, he didn't mind standing around to listen all *that* much.

"Now, you four . . ." said Ms. Grant and pointed to Brooks and his sidekicks, who had stopped a few feet away when they realized Brooks was getting in trouble.

"You four," she repeated, "are not allowed to play basketball on this court for one month. When that month is over, if you still want to play basketball, then you will have to find a way to share the court. Do you understand?"

"Yes, ma'am," all four mumbled in reply.

"Also, Brooks," said Ms. Grant. "Since I arrive on duty at the same time all of you are

coming out to recess, I think your idea is not entirely a bad one. I could use some help around the playground. For the next two weeks, you may help me set out equipment and clean up around the playground at the beginning of each recess."

Ms. Grant motioned to Brooks and his buddies.

"There's still a little time left in recess. You four may go sit by the wall near the door until it is time to go inside."

"The four of you," she said, turning to L'il Dobber, Joe, Gan, and Sam, "would enjoy playing some basketball, I believe."

The four friends smiled at one another when Brooks and his buddies walked away. They were thrilled to step back onto their court.

"What should we play first?" Sam asked.

"Definitely two-on-two," said Joe.

"Good idea," said L'il Dobber.

"Yeah. We haven't had a good game in weeks!" said Gan.

"But we can play today!" said Sam.

"And the next day!" Joe said.

"And every day!" said L'il Dobber. They all jumped into a group high-five at the center of the small court.

Chapter 9
Acting Like Dit

The Como Park bleachers were packed with the biggest crowd of any Saturday so far this season. Dit had been on the court for three games, but this fourth game was a struggle for his team. When the other team hit fifteen points, Dit was done for the day.

"Who's got next?" a player on the winning team yelled toward the bleachers.

Six new players walked onto the court. Two of them were Clyde Alexander and Zelly Dow.

"You guys got six people here," said a player on the winning team. "Someone needs to sit down."

"I made number five for this team," said Clyde. "Who came after me?"

The six guys looked at one another and then Zelly Dow spoke up.

"I came at the same time as Clyde, and I'm not waiting," he said. "I'm playing now."

The players on the court stared at Zelly. Then they all started to laugh.

"Are you serious?" Clyde asked Zelly.

"You bet."

"Am I going to have to teach you a lesson about the park?" asked Clyde. He wasn't laughing anymore.

"What lesson is that? I'm sure I know it already."

"Next is next," Clyde said and took two steps closer to Zelly. "Now get back to the bleachers."

"*I'm* playing this game," Zelly said and stepped closer to Clyde.

The unusual silence on the court made everyone in the park stop what they were doing.

L'il Dobber was getting nervous seeing

the two men in each other's faces. He didn't want to see anyone start fighting.

The bleachers were emptying. Everyone crowded around the court, hoping to see a fight. They were yelling remarks to Zelly and Clyde as the two stared at each other.

"Don't back down, Zelly."

"He's dissing you, Clyde."

"Clyde, I wouldn't take that, man."

The crowd was closing in, and L'il Dobber was getting pushed nearer and nearer to

Clyde and Zelly. He definitely did not want to be so close if they started throwing punches.

L'il Dobber glanced up at Clyde's eyes and thought for sure he saw a look that meant Clyde was going to strike.

At that instant, Dit grabbed Clyde's shoulders from behind and pulled him back a step to whisper in his ear. After Dit finished whispering, he slowly released his grip on Clyde's shoulder.

Clyde smiled with understanding. He stared at Zelly for a moment before tossing the ball at him. Then he turned and followed Dit through the crowd.

L'il Dobber was stunned motionless for a second. Then he clutched his basketball to his side and ran across the park to catch up with his dad.

I can't believe Dit stopped a fight from happening, thought L'il Dobber.

Clyde Alexander and Dit were standing by the car having a relaxed conversation when L'il Dobber finally caught up.

"Good playing today," Clyde said, smiling at Dit.

"You, too," Dit answered. "And you did a good thing leaving the court."

"It was hard to walk away, but you were right," Clyde said.

"How about some of that sweet potato pie?" asked Dit.

"Wouldn't miss it!" said Clyde.

"See ya in a few then," said Dit and climbed into the car beside L'il Dobber.

L'il Dobber and Dit drove away from the park in silence.

L'il Dobber, who was still amazed, finally had to ask, "Dit, what did you whisper to Mr. Alexander?"

"I told him I was heading home for some of your mom's sweet potato pie and he should come with me."

"What does pie have to do with basketball?" asked L'il Dobber.

"Nothing. But it cooled him down for a minute and he realized he shouldn't be fighting."

"I'm glad," said L'il Dobber. "But everyone else wanted to see them fight."

"They did. But I think a lot of people will end up respecting him for walking away," said Dit.

"I'm glad you stopped them, Dit."

Dit turned his head and smiled at his son. L'il Dobber smiled back. There didn't seem to be anything else important to say about the park games today.

During the ride home, L'il Dobber thought about how he always wanted to play ball just like his dad. But today he realized that acting like Dit included a whole lot more than just shooting hoops.

Tell us about your next adventure!

STUCK IN THE MIDDLE

Later that day, Ms. Wilson sent L'il Dobber on an errand. He had to get some books from the main office. As he walked quietly along, he saw a group of girls come out of the bathroom up ahead. Sam and Sarah were two of them. They didn't notice L'il Dobber and he was about to say hi until he heard what they were talking about.

"Why won't you come over to my house after school?" Brittany Benson, a small brown-haired girl in Mr. Martin's class was asking

Sam. "We're going to make friendship brace-lets."

"I'd love to come, but . . . well, I've got basketball practice," Sam answered hesi-tantly. "The big game is coming up."

"I told you not to go to those starting lineup tryouts," said Mindy Wasserman, an-other one of Sam's classmates. She flipped her long red hair back over her shoulder.

"Now we'll never get to see you." Brittany chimed in. "You'll be the only girl out there with all of those boys."

Sarah disagreed. "I think it's *great* that you made it, Sam."

"Great?" Mindy asked. "Now she'll be practicing even more. Sam will *never* have time to hang out with the girls."

"Mindy is right," echoed Brittany, elbow-ing Sam gently in the arm. "You'll miss all the fun. Or don't you like being one of the girls, Sam?" she asked.

"Oh, I do," Sam said. "I love hanging out with you. It's just that . . ."

"It's just . . . *what?*" asked Mindy.

"It's just that I love basketball, too," Sam explained.

"You should watch her play sometime," Sarah told the girls. "Sam is really talented."

The girls turned right down the hallway. L'il Dobber watched them go, thinking about what he'd heard. Thanks to those girls, Sam was stuck in the middle between her girl-friends and basketball.

He wondered which she would choose.

About the Authors

Bob Lanier is a basketball legend and a member of the Basketball Hall of Fame. A graduate of St. Bonaventure University, he has been hailed as much for his work in the community as for his play on the court. Winner of numerous awards and honors, he currently serves as Special Assistant to NBA Commissioner David Stern and as Captain of the NBA's All-Star Reading Team.

Like L'il Dobber, Bob has faced life's challenges head-on with a positive attitude and a never-ending belief in the power and value of reading and education.

Bob and his wife, Rose, have eight children and reside in Scottsdale, Arizona.

Heather Goodyear started creative writing in the first grade, with poems she wrote on scraps of paper. Her teacher gave her a blank notebook and said, "Be sure to let me know when you publish your first book." Hey L'il D! is her first series.

Sports were an important part of Heather's childhood in Michigan. As the only girl in a close family with two brothers, she learned early on to hold her own in living room wrestling matches, driveway basketball contests, and family football games.

Heather says that this love of sports, and her classroom experience as a teacher, makes Hey L'il D! especially fun for her to write.

Heather lives in Arizona with her husband, Chris, and their three young children.